Somebody thought it would be a good idea to bring me kayaking. This someone is at least a head taller than me, is a great swimmer, and doesn't have an irrational fear of water.

Just like everybody else in the group.

If I survive this trip, I might need a new group of friends.

# R.W. WALLACE
## AUTHOR OF THE TOLOSA MYSTERY SERIES

Being short *can* be an advantage...

# SIZE MATTERS

## AN ADVENTUROUS SHORT STORY

Size Matters

by R.W. Wallace

Copyright © 2019 by R.W. Wallace

Copy editing by Jinxie Gervasio

Cover by the author

All characters and events in this book, other than those clearly in the public domain, are fictitious and any resemblance to real persons, living or dead, is purely coincidental.

All rights reserved. No part of this publication may be reproduced, distributed, or transmitted in any form or by any means, including photocopying, recording, or other electronic or mechanical methods, without the prior written permission of the publisher, except in the case of brief quotations embodied in critical reviews and certain other noncommercial uses permitted by copyright law. For permission requests, write to the publisher, addressed "Attention: Permissions Coordinator," at the address below.

www.rwwallace.com

ISBN: [979-10-95707-25-7]

Main category—Fiction
Other category—Adventure

First Edition

14 13 12 11 10 / 10 9 8 7 6 5 4 3 2 1

# Also by R.W. Wallace

## Mystery

### The Tolosa Mystery Series
*The Red Brick Haze* (free)
*The Red Brick Cellars*

### Ghost Detective Shorts (coming soon)
*Just Desserts*
*Lost Friends*
*Family Bonds*
*Till Death*
*Common Ground*

### Short Stories
*Hidden Horrors*
*Critters*
*Gertrude and the Trojan Horse*
*First Impressions*
*Let Them Eat Cake*
*Out of Sight*
*Two's Company*

## Science Fiction (short stories)
*The Vanguard*
*Quarantine (Lollapalooza)*
*Common Enemies (Lollapalooza)*

## Adventure (short stories)
*Size Matters*

## Urban Fantasy (short stories)
*Unexpected Consequences*

# SIZE MATTERS

"*A L'ABORDAGE!*"

The expression brings to mind screaming pirates, glinting swords, high seas, and caskets of gold. It is, supposedly, what the French pirates of the good old days screamed when they attacked other ships.

Today, it's a little less violent, though no less scary.

Pierre and Eric, my fiancé Lucas' best friends, have decided that the part of the river we're currently kayaking on, is too boring. Instead of staying on their kayak like normal, sensible people, and enjoying the pretty scenery, they're standing up in their seats, paddles abandoned by their feet as if they weren't the only tool that would allow them to get home safely.

Pierre is the "small" guy of our group. I put the word in quotes because he's still a good head taller than me. Everybody is. But compared to the other guys, he's short and skinny. I never quite understood how he'd managed to integrate a group like this, where everybody else is twice his size, either from playing rugby, basket, or volleyball, or—in Eric's case—as a result of having giant blood running through his veins. Pierre reaches to about shoulder-height of all his friends, has never lifted a weight or touched a ball in his life, and can't weigh more than fifty-five kilos soaking wet. Which he will be shortly.

I figured the guys were just being their usual goofy selves, and would only put themselves in danger, but no. They have to bring everyone else into their folly, too. Once mine and Lucas' kayak arrive alongside theirs, Pierre screams his war-cry and jumps at Lucas.

I kid you not, he *jumps* from one kayak to another. In the middle of the river. With who knows how much water and rocks below him.

He misses, but that's beside the point.

I can't believe I'm here in the first place.

This weekend is supposed to be our combined hen's night/bachelor party. We decided to do it together since I have more male friends than female and it just felt unfair that I'd go out partying with two friends, and Lucas got do to fun stuff with his *and* my friends. So we figured we'd have fun together.

I'd like to know who thought *water* would be fun. I'm pretty sure everyone knows I'm afraid of water—have been since my uncle literally threw into the deep end of the pool when I was little—and yet they figured an entire day on a boat that's closer to being a stick than anything else, going down a river riddled with *rapids*, with everyone dunking each other and *frolicking* in the water, would be something I'd like.

Lucas realized the problem immediately, of course. (And a good thing, too, or I just might have called off the wedding.) He offered to share a kayak with me, with him in the back steering. It went a good way toward reassuring me—until I realized our mistake. This *is* his bachelor party. So his friends are honor-bound to make him suffer in some way.

Which means I'm ideally placed to become collateral damage.

Like right now. With Pierre mid-air between our kayaks, his skinny limbs making me think of monkeys jumping from tree to tree, I'm seeing the world in slow motion.

He's going to land on Lucas. Pierre is going to break something, like an arm or a leg, when he hits our kayak. He's going to head-butt Lucas, making them both disoriented. Lucas is going to lose his paddle, which is going to ride away on the current, leaving us with only one paddle for two. They're both going to fall into the water, where they're going to hit rocks (the guy we rented the kayaks from explained this to us in great detail, about how much it can hurt to hit a rock with your foot while you're pulled along by the current) and probably break another limb. Maybe Lucas will be confused by the hit to the head, and won't know up from down, and will end up drowning right before my eyes.

Pierre misses his mark by almost a meter. He barely manages to hit our kayak with one hand, then the whole guy disappears into the river with a surprisingly small splash.

He doesn't even really go under before the life vest pulls him back up. Everybody hoots in laughter as Pierre sputters.

I manage a small chuckle, because Pierre has gone from flying monkey to wet dog, and it somehow suits him. With his longish, curly dark hair flat against his skull, he looks pitiful in a cute kind of way.

Another, "*A l'abordage!*" sounds, this time with considerably more volume.

I snap my head around, to see that Eric has maneuvered their kayak around to our other side, so close there's hardly a hand's breadth between the two vessels. He's standing in his seat, towering above Lucas' head, his arms spread out, making him look like a freakishly big Jesus without the cross.

He jumps.

Lands chest-first just behind Lucas with an *oof*.

Like I said, Eric's a big guy. At least two meters, wide shoulders, solid bones, a weirdly huge amount of muscles for someone who never works out, and a not so weird amount of fat. When a guy like that lands on the very tip of a kayak? And when, at the other end of the kayak, you have a girl who's about a quarter of his weight?

The girl learns to fly.

I'm ejected out of the kayak. I have the time to see Lucas' surprised expression as I pass overhead, and hear Pierre exclaim, "Shit!" Then I hit the water.

It's cold.

It's wet.

It's *everywhere*.

I can't figure out what's up and what's down. I can't draw breath. I flail about with both arms and legs but can't find purchase anywhere.

A pair of hands grab me under the arms and pull me up.

I draw a deep breath, then another.

I'm held up by the strong arms while my arms and legs are still flailing.

"It's not deep," a voice says behind me. I think it's Pierre. "Just get your legs under you, and you'll be fine. You can do it, Julie."

"I can't," I say, gasping in yet another breath. "I'm too short."

Pierre chuckles. "I know you're short, Julie, but the water barely reaches my waist. If you just manage to get your legs vertical instead of horizontal, you'll be fine."

I come out of my panic for long enough to actually look up at him. He's standing behind me, holding me with both arms. The water reaches his waist.

I follow his instructions, and seconds later I'm standing on my own two feet.

"Don't leave," I tell him and grab onto his life vest. The water might not be deep, but it's *moving*. Not as quickly as in the rapids we passed earlier, but still enough to sweep me downstream if I lose my footing again.

"No worries," Pierre says with a kind smile. "I'm not going anywhere. Actually, I don't think any of us are moving for a while."

I follow his gaze. My jaw drops in shock.

Both kayaks have capsized. They're calmly floating past us down the river, keel up, with nobody aboard. A little farther down, a white keg bobs—the containers we got to protect our gear from water. It must not have been sufficiently secured to whichever kayak it came from.

For a second, I'm worried about our stuff, but then I remember what's more important. "Lucas!"

A groan from behind me. I whip around—while keeping a death grip on Pierre's life vest—afraid of what I'll see.

Lucas and Eric are both bobbing along on the surface of the river. Eric is in a semi-fetal position with both hands on his lower stomach, and Lucas is gingerly touching his head, bringing his hand in front of his eyes to check for blood.

Bloody idiots.

I'd like to check they're not injured too badly, but since they're still moving and talking, there's one thing that's more important right now. "All our stuff is floating away," I tell Pierre. "We have to get it!"

"We'll grab your stuff, Julie!" I hardly have time to understand what's going on before my friend Audrey has already passed us. She shares a kayak with one of Lucas' friends—Guillaume, or Vincent, or something, I can't remember—and flashes me a smile as she points toward our kayaks and the plastic container. "We'll pick everything up and wait for you on that beach down there." She points down the river, at a white spot in the middle of all the brown and green—presumably a beach.

"Thanks, Audrey!" Pierre shouts. "See?" He gives me another smile as he grabs me around the shoulders. "Your friend has your back. Now, let's have a look at these two morons." He pulls me along toward Lucas and Eric.

They've drifted closer to the bank, under the branches of a group of trees crowding the shore. Lucas has come enough to his senses to grab hold of one of the branches, and to hold back his friend with his other hand.

"Come on, Eric," he says. "Get your feet under you. I swear to God, it's like holding back a whale."

With another groan, Eric does as instructed, and soon we're all standing amongst the branches, water up to the chest in my case, almost to the hips in Eric and Lucas' case.

"Audrey's gathering up our stuff," Pierre says. "All we have to do is meet up with them a little farther down the river. I say we just swim down."

I've had enough of the water for a while, so I pull myself up on a branch that seems big enough to hold my weight. I've just found a seat where only my feet touch the water when Pierre makes his suggestion.

"No way," I say, my voice brooking no argument. "I'm not getting back in the water right now. We're not *swimming* three hundred meters in a river with that strong a current. You're going to have to come up with something else."

☙

I'M PROBABLY GOING to hear about this for years to come, but no matter what the guys propose, I'm not going back in the water. It's easy for them to say the swim will be a piece of cake. They're built like houses—except for Pierre, but he has this air about him that makes me think he can manage a lot more than you'd assume—will probably be able to touch the bottom at any time and have enough mass to fight against the pull of the current.

Lucas even proposed to carry me on his back, but I shake my head—violently. "I'm not going back in the water without a kayak. And when I do,"—I point an angry finger at all three of them—"no more boarding!"

"Fine," Lucas finally concedes. "If we can't go on the water, we'll go on land."

We all turn to look at the dense forest rising up on the bank beside us.

"There are often hiking trails along this river," Pierre offers hesitantly. "I guess we could try to find one."

"Sounds like a plan." Lucas slaps Eric on the back. "Eric, since you're the reason we're in this mess, I propose you go first."

"How gallant of you," Eric says, but he pulls aside a branch and approaches the shore.

"That's exactly what I'm planning on being," Lucas says, then wades over to the branch I'm sitting on. He puts a calming hand on my thigh and fixes me with his beautiful brown eyes. "I'm really sorry about this, *chérie*. Want to piggyback over to the bank?"

Smiling for the first time in what feels like forever, I give him a quick kiss on the lips. "Thank you." I climb onto his back and sling my arms around his shoulders. I get a whiff of his familiar cologne and the warmth of his skin against my cheek erases my remaining stress.

Ahead of us, Eric leads the way with a string of curses. The positive thing with having a mountain leading the way is that if he gets through, we'll get through, too.

We don't find a path. What we do find, is a steep climb, lots of rocks, and a cave.

"Now what?" Eric asks Lucas as his gaze shifts from me to the cave.

"What do you say, Julie?" Lucas asks, hitching me higher up his back. He doesn't really need to carry me anymore, but as long as he doesn't ask me to get down, I'm going to cling to his back like a monkey. "Back in the water, or attempt through the cave?"

The mouth of the cave doesn't look too impressive. It's maybe two meters high and three across and turns completely black after only a meter or two.

"Is there any chance of it having another opening farther down the bank?" I ask. I glance back in the direction we came from, with the murky, swirling water and the low, treacherous branches.

"These hills are riddled with caves." Pierre shrugs. "Anything's possible."

Not exactly a ringing endorsement, but I'm only going back in the water if it's the only option available. "Let's try the cave."

⌘

I THINK WE all realize quickly that going into the cave wasn't a bright idea. But I'm too scared of going back into the water to propose turning back, and the guys are…guys.

"I can't see a thing," Pierre says in the darkness. "As long as there's open space in front of me, I keep going. Let's just hope I don't step into a hole or anything." He laughs as if that would be hilarious, not deathly dangerous. "Eric, watch your head, okay? Just because I don't hit anything doesn't mean you won't."

"No worries here," Eric says from just in front of me. "I'm keeping one hand in front of my face and one on your ass."

"That's my head."

Eric chuckles. "Same difference."

I hold onto the back of Eric's life vest as if my life depends on it, and the other in front of my face. Even if Eric should detect any issues by walking right in front of me, I just can't walk in complete darkness and not protect my face. Behind me, Lucas holds onto my vest.

"Man, what I wouldn't give for a phone right now," Eric says. "What did people do without phones? Always walk around in the dark?"

"There's this thing called a flashlight," Pierre says. "It's really—"

He cuts himself off with a sharp intake of breath. There's a splash, followed by a curse.

"You all right, Pierre?" Lucas asks from behind me.

More cursing. "I'm fine," Pierre finally replies. "Found myself a hole to step in, is all."

I instinctively lean to the side to speak around Eric, though it won't help me see Pierre. "Anything hurt?"

"Nah." I hear more splashing. "Ankle's not thrilled, but I don't think it's sprained or anything."

"There's water?" I hate how small my voice sounds.

"Not too much," is the quick reply. "It hardly covers my ankle. Do we continue?" Pierre asks after a brief pause.

Lucas' voice sounds distant. He must be talking into the dark behind us. "At this point, I don't think we have much of a choice," he says. "Or rather, might as well, since I'm not sure we can be sure to find the same way back out."

Great. "Forward it is, then." My voice sounds almost normal.

We all splash into the water and the ground starts to slope downward. The bottom is soft, probably sand, so the footing's good, but for every step, the water comes a little higher. Before long, it reaches my thighs, and I abandon trying to protect my head and place my second hand on top of Lucas', making sure he won't let go.

He squeezes my hand, and we continue forward.

༄

When the water reaches my waist, I want to ask whose idea it was to go into the cave. I keep quiet, of course, since it's all my fault. If I'd accepted to go back into the river, we wouldn't be here.

Pierre stops, and the rest of us follow suit.

"I think I might be hallucinating," he says. "I see light."

I lean out to see past Eric, and I see it, too. Some way ahead, there's a sprinkling of lights, like stars covering the sky at night.

"It feels like we've been here forever," Eric says from above my head somewhere. "But I don't think it should be dark out just yet."

"It's glowworms." Stepping very carefully, I walk past Eric, transferring my iron grip on his vest onto Pierre's. I can actually see the outline of his head where he's blocking the view of the worms. "Let's go check them out."

"Okay." There's doubt in Pierre's voice. "But we're going to have to swim. The bottom seems to fall away just a step ahead."

I gulp so loudly I'm sure the whole group hears it.

"The vests will keep us afloat, *chérie*," Lucas says. "And we'll stay together. You know none of us will do anything stupid now, right? No joking around."

Eric and Pierre agree, making me realize how obvious my fear must be. If we ever get out of here alive, I'm finding out who came up with the idea of kayaking, and uninviting him or her from the wedding. Possibly cutting all contact forever.

"I'll come swim next to you," Lucas says. "We'll have Pierre up front and Eric in the back. You'll be fine."

I reluctantly agree, mostly because I don't have a choice. We need to find a way out of here and going past a living organism seems like a good idea, somehow.

I float on my back, concentrating only on not drowning, while Lucas swims by my side, pulling me along.

When we reach the glowworms, some of my fear eases into awe. It's so pretty. If I unfocus my eyes a little, it's like I'm under the open sky, looking up at thousands of twinkling stars.

Something furry touches my face.

I screech and try folding into a ball with my hands covering my face. I sink deeper into the water, making my panic go up a notch. "What was that?" I scream. "Something touched my face! Lucas!"

Strong arms fold around my body and Lucas' voice is in my ear. "Shh, *chérie*. You're fine. I'm here." There's some sort of flapping over our heads. "Is that—"

The flapping multiplies all around us, creating a breeze on my face.

"Bats," Eric says from behind us. "A lot of them." Even *more* flapping. "I'd advise getting as close to the water as possible until they calm down."

I give up on trying to maintain any shred of dignity and pull my face against Lucas' chest. He places us so his body protects me from the increasingly active bats, and we stay this way for several minutes. I think we might be drifting, but it's not even that big of a deal, as long as the four of us stay together.

We're as lost as you can get—what's a minute or two of drifting going to change?

Eventually, silence returns.

"I think they're all gone." There's some splashing as I assume Pierre moves around a bit to test the waters.

"Now what?" Lucas asks the question, but nobody answers.

I wonder how long it will take our friends to realize we're lost and send a search party after us. Will they find the cave?

Would it be better for us to keep moving, or to stay put?

A bark comes from somewhere far to my left.

"What was that?" Eric says.

"Sounded like a dog," Pierre replies.

"I vote we go check it out," Eric says and I can feel him moving toward the sound, dragging us along behind him.

"I agree," I say. Doing my best to ignore the fact that I'm in the dark, in water so deep even Eric's feet don't touch the bottom, I swim alongside the guys. I can't rely on Lucas for everything. Time to be a big girl.

The guys call out to the dog as they swim, and the dog seems to hear them. Its barking intensifies, sounding excited.

Pierre bumps his head a couple of times and we all have chattering teeth from the cold water, but we end up reaching the dog.

"Ouch!" Pierre exclaims. "It's on dry ground. Looks like we're done swimming for the time being."

Thank God. I hurry forward and feel an unnatural level of relief at having solid ground under my hands and feet again.

Right now, I don't even care if we make it out of the cave, so long as I don't have to get back into the water.

"What are you doing here, big guy?" Pierre asks.

The dog barks in reply.

"Wanna go that way, do you? Show the way. We'll follow."

Guess we're following the dog.

This time, there's no water, but there's also not a lot of space. We crawl along on all fours and since there are times when even I knock into the rock above us, I can only imagine what this must be like for Eric and Lucas. But nobody complains, as we pray the dog is showing us the exit.

After a time, it suddenly dawns on me that I can see the feet of Eric in front of me. Not more than an outline, but it's infinitely better than what we've had since we stepped into this hell-hole. "Where's the light coming from?" I ask.

"Up ahead," Eric replies and there's excitement in his voice. "There seems to be some sort of chamber."

The dog is yapping like crazy and it's not long until the narrow tunnel opens up, and we're crawling into a bigger space. I realize there's another voice here, too.

Against the wall, sitting in a ray of light falling down from above, as if taken out of some story from the Bible, a dark-haired guy is scratching the ears of the dog. I'm going to go with Labrador Retriever, but dogs aren't really my thing, so I could be wrong.

The dog is all excited, but the man seems to be in bad shape. His right leg is clearly broken and bent at an unnatural angle, and from the swelling on his left ankle, I'm going to guess it's at least sprained.

"Good boy," the man says to his dog, his voice weak. "Good boy." He looks up at us with weary eyes. Takes in our bathing shorts and life vests. Pierre's banged-up forehead. Stares at my face for a while, making me wonder to what extent my fear is showing.

"I was kind of hoping for a rescue team," he says. "But you guys will do. I'm Bertrand."

"We were kind of hoping your dog was the rescue team," Pierre counters, his lips lifted in a sad smile.

The man—Bertrand—sighs. "He's halfway there, I think. He keeps trying to get me to follow him down there." He points across the chamber to the opening of another tunnel. "But when I don't follow, he just comes back here."

He perks up a little, winces in pain. "Maybe he can lead you guys out, then you can get some help back here."

Eric grunts and walks over to the tunnel to check it out. "What happened to you, anyway?" he throws over his shoulder.

Bertrand looks up, making me think of the Bible again with the sun streaming down on his strained and tired face. "Fell through the roof."

We all look up. The sun is coming through a hole in the rocks, perhaps ten meters above us. It's big enough for a man to fall through. We measure the drop with our eyes, then look to his ruined legs.

Lucas goes over to the wounded man to see if he can help with the pain in any way, but I stay put. I don't do too well around blood. I study the walls around us, but don't see any way for us to climb up and out without risking our necks.

"This tunnel is tiny," Eric says. His voice is distant since he has his head inside the opening. Indeed, there's no way for him to fit in there, let alone manage to move once he's in. He backs up then studies Pierre and myself with narrowed eyes. "You guys might fit."

Shrugging, Pierre walks over. "I'll give it a try." He crouches down on all fours and crawls forward. He disappears from view, but mere minutes later he's crawling back out ass first.

"It narrows even more after a few meters," he says. His gaze locks with mine. "You might fit, though."

Legs shaking, I make it over to where Eric and Pierre are studying the tunnel.

"Can't see any light," Eric says.

"No, but it's not completely dark, either," Pierre says. "When I had to turn around, I basically blocked all the light from here, and I could still see."

I crouch down. I can see where the tunnel's going for about five or six meters before it veers to the left, out of sight. The spot where it narrows is about halfway in.

"What if it leads nowhere?" I ask, trying to imagine going in there all alone. "What if it narrows down again? What if there's water?"

Bertrand speaks up, his voice strained as Lucas is trying to set his leg. "I don't think there's any water. My dog's been through there several times already, and he's been dry the entire time."

I face the tunnel, picturing myself in there. Can I do it? Can I manage my fear and not have a panic attack in a place where nobody can reach me?

Do I really have a choice?

"I'll do it."

☙

It took some time for Bertrand to convince his dog to leave him and take me instead. When I said I'm not into dogs, that clearly goes both ways. But in the end, we manage, and the blonde dog sets off down the tunnel ahead of me.

Right now, I'm a few meters after the narrowing spot, and my head, shoulders, and knees all touch the rock walls around me. I *just* have enough space to wiggle forward, centimeter by centimeter.

The dog runs back and forth, making sure I'm following, giving me little licks of encouragement whenever my breathing gets too panicky. I may have judged the species too quickly in the past.

We pass the turn and though I haven't seen my friends since I entered this wormhole, I know that now, they can't see me, either.

Pierre was right, though. There's light. It's coming from up ahead, and it can't be that far off.

So I hunker down and crawl forward, focusing only on taking the next step, and on taking comfort from the dog whenever he offers it. I even give him a scratch in return when I can manage it.

After what feels like an eternity, I turn another bend, and see direct sunlight. A couple of happy tears streak down my cheek. The dog comes to lick them away. Laughing, I'm tempted to lick him right back.

I scurry out the rest of the way, and a minute later I'm free. I stand up straight and stretch, then bend down to scratch the dog's ears. "Good boy," I tell him.

I might be out free, but my friends and poor Bertrand are still stuck in the cave. They're going to need help to get out, either the way we came in, or through the hole in the ceiling.

I study the area around me, trying to take note of where I am. I don't want to lose the entrance. I don't find anything particularly helpful, but I do spot some color not too far away. Squinting, I make out at least eight people, all wearing the same life vests as me, and six red things that are probably kayaks.

My friends! I start jumping up and down, waving my arms, screaming my head off. Not long after, they see me, and a group of three sets off to meet me when it becomes clear I'm not coming to them.

The dog yaps happily as he runs back and forth between my legs and the tunnel opening. "You wanna go back to Bertrand?" I ask him as I crouch down and give him a hug. "You go ahead. I've got it from here."

He hesitates for a second, but when he sees I'm not stopping him from going back in, he gives me one last lick, then speeds down the tunnel.

I sit down on the ground and try to get my limbs to stop shaking.

☙

THEY ENDED UP pulling everyone out through the hole in the roof. Turns out, it was quite large and could take both Eric's wide shoulders and Bertrand with his leg in a makeshift cast.

The rescue team asked if we wanted to be brought home, but we had kayaks to return. The rental company probably could have come get them later, but that would mean admitting we'd done something really stupid. If we brought them in ourselves—even if we'd be about five hours late—we'd only have done something a little stupid.

This does mean, however, that I have to get back on the thing.

"You want me to ride with you again?" Lucas asks as I stand contemplating the evil contraption that is a kayak.

"Yes," I reply. "But you have to promise there won't be a single drop of water splashed my way. No boarding. No shenanigans. Or I'm filing for divorce."

Lucas laughs. "I promise. But you can't ask for a divorce when we're not even married yet."

I give him a mock glare. "Try me. I'll marry you, take all the gifts, and divorce you for half of everything. Just you watch."

Lucas raises his arms in surrender. "Not a drop of water, I promise."

"Good." I nod, brace myself, and step into the water to gingerly slide into my seat at the front of the kayak. That wasn't so bad.

"Anything you want, *chérie*." Lucas shoves us into the river and the kayak wobbles as he takes his seat.

"Excellent." I lean back in my seat with my arms crossed. One of the paddles were lost in the boarding earlier, and I've decided I can do just as well without it.

"By the way," I say to the setting sun. "We're getting a dog."

# THANK YOU

THANK YOU FOR reading *Size Matters*. I hope you enjoyed it!

If you liked the story, you might want to check out some of my other books mentioned on the next page. It's mostly Mysteries, but a few other genres will pop up, too.

And don't forget that the first book of my *Tolosa Mystery* series, *The Red Brick Haze*, is available for free on my website.

*R.W. Wallace*
www.rwwallace.com

# Also by R.W. Wallace

## Mystery

### The Tolosa Mystery Series
*The Red Brick Haze* (free)
*The Red Brick Cellars*

### Ghost Detective Shorts (coming soon)
*Just Desserts*
*Lost Friends*
*Family Bonds*
*Till Death*
*Common Ground*

### Short Stories
*Hidden Horrors*
*Critters*
*Gertrude and the Trojan Horse*
*First Impressions*
*Let Them Eat Cake*
*Out of Sight*
*Two's Company*

## Science Fiction (short stories)
*The Vanguard*
*Quarantine (Lollapalooza)*
*Common Enemies (Lollapalooza)*

## Adventure (short stories)
*Size Matters*

## Urban Fantasy (short stories)
*Unexpected Consequences*

www.ingramcontent.com/pod-product-compliance
Lightning Source LLC
LaVergne TN
LVHW041603070526
838199LV00047B/2115